Oxford University Press, Walton Street, Oxford OX2 6DP

Oxford is a trade mark of Oxford University Press

© Editions Fontanille, contes en diapositives, Meudon, 1982
© Gautier-Languereau, 1990
English version © Oxford University Press, 1991
First published in France as *Tout Seuls!*
First published in the UK by Oxford University Press, 1991
First published in paperback, 1993
Reprinted in paperback with new cover, 1996
All rights reserved

A CIP catalogue record for this book is available
from the British Library

ISBN 0 19 272268 9 paperback

Printed in Hong Kong

Michel Gay & Monique Ponty

All Alone
~ at Christmas ~

English text by Michiel Timmerman and Marilyn Watts

Oxford University Press

It's nearly Christmas. In the shop window, we've been waiting for days . . .

hoping someone will take us home.

It's not much fun, waiting. Some of us leave, while others stay behind. I'm just a little white kitten, and I'm scared I'll be forgotten, because I'm so small.

The big bear is scared, too. He has one blue eye and one brown eye, and he's afraid that no one will ever buy him, because of his odd eyes.

Sometimes people stop in the street outside. Then they come in
and ask to look at me.

But no one ever buys me. They always choose the others.

The big bear says that people are strange. They like the look of you, they pick you up . . . and then they change their minds.

Now the lion has been bought, too. Soon there will be only the
big bear and me left in the window.

I can't stand waiting any more. I'm going to leave, too.
— What, all alone? In the middle of the night?

Do you think we'll be all right in the world outside?

Careful, Bear! You're knocking everything over.

Mind the train!

Oh look! It's beautiful out here.
It's so soft, but very cold.

These huge cars frighten me.
— Don't be afraid. It's safe on the pavement.

Let's run for a bit, to warm us up.

Wait for me! You're going too fast, and I'm tired.

I'll carry you, then. Look at the weather — it's snowing harder
and harder.

I'm cold, and I'm scared. I want to go back to our shop.
— All right . . . but I think we're lost.

Do you think that tomorrow morning we'll be able to find our way back?

What are you two doing, all alone? You'll freeze if you stay there.
Come on, I'm going to take you home with me.

Here we are. We've found someone to love us, and a real home.

And look, it's Christmas!